Not Quite A Blessing

Emily Martha Sorensen

Also by Emily Martha Sorensen

Wicked Witches of Restva:
Black Magic Academy
White Magic Academy

The End in the Beginning:
The Keeper and the Rulership
The Fires of the Rulership
The Magic or the Rulership

Fairy Senses:
Fairy Eyeglasses
Fairy Compass
Fairy Earmuffs
Fairy Barometer
Fairy Pox
Fairy Slippers
Fairy Lunchbox
Fairy Icepack
Fairy Stopwatch
Fairy Toothbrush
Fairy Perfume
Fairy Crown

Dragon Eggs:
Dragon's Egg
Dragon's Hope
Dragon's First Christmas
Dragon's Fire
Dragon's Song
Dragon's First Valentine

Comics:
A Magical Roommate
To Prevent World Peace

The Numbers Just Keep
Getting Bigger:
Twenty-Four Potential
Children of Prophecy

Trilogy of a Teenage Werevulture:
Trials of a Teenage Werevulture
Trifles of a Teenage Werevulture

Weredodo Cozy Mysteries:
Weredodo Sleuth

The Virgo Curse:
Not Quite a Curse

Magical Mayhem:
To Prevent World Peace
To Prevent Chic Costumes
To Prevent Clear Paths
To Prevent Smart Choices
To Prevent Warm Welcomes
To Prevent Cute Mascots
To Prevent First Place (prologue)
To Prevent Fresh Starts
To Prevent New Allies
To Prevent Best Friends
To Prevent Good Luck

Short Story Collections:
Worlds of Wonder
Magic and Mischief
Tales of Tie-Ins

Picture Books:
Tabby, Tabby, Burning Bright

http://www.emilymarthasorensen.com

To all the authors of shoujo manga
who have given me
loads of enjoyment over the years.

You know what inspired this book.

Chapter 1

Not Quite Allured

Tapping her pencil against the side of her face, Lucy eyed the back of the guy who was sitting in front of her.

Alex really is attractive, she thought, an impish grin spreading across her face. *Shame about the personality, but he's sure cute. Those strong arms, and his hair . . .*

Those arms tensed, as did the neck above them.

Lucy giggled softly. *Did I just make him fall for me? Whoops! Didn't mean to do that. Those dates he took me on last year were a total snore. He's sooooooo boring. Still, I mean . . . he is really cute. Maybe I could give him a third date, after all . . .*

"Time's up," the teacher called from the front of the room. "Hand in your tests."

Lucy sighed loudly and slammed her pencil on the desk. She hated math, and tests were the worst part of all. Not only were they actually more boring than lectures, which was ridiculous because the lectures were a snore, she knew she'd failed the whole thing again. She probably hadn't even gotten one question right. Which meant a math tutor again, which meant no Fridays . . .

Something sharp poked her in the back, and Lucy jumped, turning to see the jealous-looking girl behind her had poked her with the sharp end of her pencil. Lucy had a lot of enemies at the moment, because all the unattached cute boys at school kept falling for her.

Smirking knowingly at the jealous girl, Lucy took the stack of test papers and added her own to it. Then, noting with approval the adorable little curl right behind Alex's ear, she tapped him on the shoulder.

He turned around, his expression flat, as usual. "Stop it."

"I'm just passing you the papers."

"That's not what I meant," Alex said, reaching for them.

"Then what'd you mean?" she demanded.

"You know what." He passed the stack forward to the student ahead of him.

"No, I don't."

He sighed heavily. "Stop thinking about me, Lucy."

Her mouth fell open. "You don't get to be my thought police!"

"I do when you affect *my* thoughts," he shot back. "There's such a thing as self-control. Use it."

Lucy slouched back against the back of her chair, indignant. *It's not my fault boys fall in love with me when I'm attracted to them! Besides, there has to be something good about this dumb curse!*

The Virgo curse was sort of hereditary, and she was the current bearer of it. The way it worked was that it would keep messing with her head, trying to turn her personality into the ideal Virgo, until it finally succeeded and then she died. Talk about gag.

Alex was cursed, too. That was why he knew how her power worked, and that it even existed. Her curse was Virgo, and his was Gemini. Their curses worked the same way, only the power his gave him was different. If she remembered right, he could read his twin's mind or something.

The bell rang, and everyone gathered up their books and stood from their desks.

"Hey, how long've you been — y'know?" Lucy asked Alex.

Not Quite Allured

"I don't know what you're talking about." He tucked his books neatly into the backpack beside his chair.

Lucy smacked her hand on her desk. "You know exactly what I'm talking about! It's the word I can't say!"

That was another annoying thing about the curse. It kept you from talking about it directly.

"Oh, that," Alex said, his voice perfectly level. He looked up. "My father died when I was two months old."

Lucy's breath caught in her throat. *When . . . you were . . .?*

Forget the fact that his father must have been the last Gemini, which was bad enough. Lucy couldn't imagine losing a parent to the curse and then inheriting it. She'd only lost her Aunt Aggie, a person she hadn't known well or cared about all that much. Alex had been cursed since he was *two months old?*

She couldn't help doing the math instantly, even though she couldn't stand math. The longest anyone had ever lived after inheriting a zodiac curse was twenty years.

"Aren't you seventeen now?" she asked.

"Yeah." His rueful smile answered the unspoken question.

Lucy stared at him in horror. That meant he had less than three years to live?! Ugh! Cute was cute, but . . . man, that was way too short!

Maybe she'd feel differently if she'd been cursed for a long time herself, but she'd only just inherited her curse a few weeks ago. She hoped to live for twenty more years, at least. Heck, she wanted to set a new record and go for a hundred.

Alex looked both slightly amused and a bit sad. He'd probably seen that look a dozen times before, anytime a person who knew about the curses realized how long he had left.

Lucy swallowed. She felt like a total heel. So what if he didn't have that long left? She could be nice to him. She could go out on dates with him. He was really cute, and it wasn't like a few dates in high school was a lifetime commitment . . .

"Lucy," Alex said gently but firmly. "Stop it."

"But —" Lucy protested.

"I mean it. Turn your attentions to somebody else, please."

Then he picked up his bag and left.

Lucy picked up her hated math textbook and followed him out into the hallway, her usual enthusiasm dampened. She'd felt so sorry for herself for being cursed, but man, some people had it way worse. Even if turning her down was kind of jerky . . .

"Hi, gorgeous Lucy!" Pablo called, waving to her from across the hallway. "We still on for Saturday?"

Lucy grinned, distracted. She loved what a flirt he was.

"Yeah, cutie pie!" she called.

"Hey, what about me? Aren't I cuter than him?" Brad hollered from his locker.

Lucy was about to flirt back, but then she noticed a poisonous glance being aimed in her direction.

Oh, right. He has a girlfriend, she remembered.

"Not when you have a girlfriend, you aren't!" she called back.

"Oooh! Burned!" his friends laughed.

For some reason, that didn't abate the girl's venom at all.

Sheesh, Ellie, lay off, Lucy thought grumpily. *It isn't my fault that my power triggers whenever I notice a guy's attractive.*

All the same, she recited to herself over and over again, *Guys who think it's okay to cheat on their girlfriends are not cute. Guys who think it's okay to cheat on their girlfriends are not cute.*

Because, for real, that wasn't an attractive trait at all. If she ever wanted to have a steady boyfriend, which she didn't right now, she would want him to be faithful. *I mean, duh.*

So, really, truly, honestly, Brad *wasn't* cute. If he was hitting on her while he was dating someone else, he was gross. As long as she could remember that, it should help.

She got stopped by three other guys on the way to her locker, all of them guys she'd absently noticed were a bit attractive at some point today, and let them fill up the rest of her week with first dates. They all seemed thrilled that she knew their names before they introduced themselves.

Yeah, but I know everybody at school's name, Lucy thought, a bit embarrassed that they probably thought that was significant. She even knew all the teachers' first names.

Not Quite Allured

She finally waded through the crowd to reach her locker, where all four of her friends were waiting. Jezza was checking her makeup in a mirror, Matilda was playing a game on her phone, Carrie had a sour look on her face, and Natasia was smooching her boyfriend Sean. Those two did not understand the concept of "not making the people around them uncomfortable."

"Oh, look, it's Lucy and her harem," Carrie said acidly.

Lucy glanced back to see five cute guys who were shyer than the ones who'd just asked her out quickly scatter. Apparently they'd been following her as she walked down the hallway.

"Good word for it," Jezza laughed. "You always make such a scene."

"Sorry," Lucy said sheepishly.

Sean and Natasia were whispering in each other's ears and ignoring the rest of them.

Sean was a weird mystery. It was a relief that he seemed to be immune to Lucy's power, since she didn't want to steal her friend Natasia's longtime boyfriend, but she didn't understand why. She definitely thought he was hot. In fact, the fact that he was so sweet to Natasia just made him more attractive, no matter how hard Lucy tried not to think of him that way.

"So what's the plan today?" Matilda asked, looking up from her phone.

"Carrie and I were talking about the mall earlier," Jezza said. "There's that earring sale you want to check out, right?"

"Yeah, but she can't go!" Carrie said quickly, glancing at Lucy.

"Huh?" Lucy stared at her. "Why not?"

"Because I like the guy who works at the hot dog place, and if he sees you, he'll fall for *you!*"

Lucy gulped. She may have accidentally attracted three of Carrie's crushes in the past two weeks.

"Okay," she said in a small voice, not wanting to start a fight. "No big deal. I have homework tonight, anyway."

Chapter 2
Not Quite Welcome

Morosely, Lucy walked out of the school building on her own.

I left the whole afternoon free to hang out with my friends, she thought, kicking a rock on the sidewalk. *And they ditched me. It's true that I have homework, but I wasn't planning to actually do it!*

Since one of the traits of a Virgo was cool-headed practicality and diligence, Lucy felt no desire whatsoever to be more responsible than usual. She'd skipped out on math homework almost every night a month ago, and she wasn't going to start changing that now, even though the thought of leaving things unfinished that she was supposed to do was starting to bug her a little.

As she walked down the sidewalk, guys she knew whistled at her and waved. She halfheartedly waved back or ignored them. Because Lucy wasn't paying attention to any strangers she passed, nobody new seemed to react to her.

A roar passed by her, and a motorbike stopped at the curb.

"Hey, Lucy!" said a guy in a helmet. He removed it, and a familiar face appeared from underneath. "Nice to meet you!"

Not Quite Welcome

"Alex?" Lucy said, baffled. This seemed unlike him.

"Nope! Try again."

"Oh!" Lucy snapped her fingers. "You're his twin, Xander! Your parents were super uncreative and gave you almost the same name!"

"That's me!" He reached into a bag by his side and pulled out a second helmet. "Here. Hop on."

Lucy stared at him. "You must be joking."

"Nope, not joking at all. C'mon. I'm cute. You like cute guys, right?" He grinned.

Lucy stared at him flatly. "I've heard about you from Alex. I don't trust you."

"What've you heard?" he asked easily.

"That you're trouble."

"Yeah, well, Alex doesn't understand me."

"He *knows what you think!*" Lucy exclaimed. Always being able to read his twin's mind was the Gemini's power.

"Doesn't mean he understands me." Xander tossed the helmet up in the air and caught it. "If your parents could read your mind constantly, would you think they understood you?"

Lucy shuddered at the idea. If her overprotective father could read her mind, he'd never let her out of the house. "Nooooo."

"There ya go." Xander held out the helmet and grinned.

"That doesn't mean I trust you!" Lucy retorted. "I've never met you before!"

"Exactly," Xander said, his eyes glinting. "That's the whole problem I'm trying to fix. C'mon. You like me, don't you? I can tell because I've got a real thing for you."

Lucy coughed and tossed her hair to stall for time. It hadn't occurred to her that a guy who knew about her power would understand what it said about her feelings.

"Well, maybe I do," she said coyly. There seemed no point in lying when he knew for a fact she did. The fact was, he was just as attractive as Alex, and she liked his flirtatious manner way more than Alex's quiet brooding. "But I'm not getting in a vehicle with a guy I just met. Especially without my dad's approval."

She had no interest in being grounded for the rest of her life if her dad found out about it.

"Okay, fine." Xander plopped on his helmet and drove off.

Lucy felt oddly crestfallen, watching him disappear around the corner. *Really? That's it?*

He'd seemed so interested, and he was so cute. She wouldn't have minded him trying to convince her for awhile longer, even though she wouldn't have told him yes.

She shook her head, adjusted her backpack, and told herself to forget the odd conversation as she kept on walking down the hill away from the school. She reached the bottom of the hill and waited for the crosswalk sign to light up. It was taking forever.

Loud footsteps came running behind her.

She spun around to see Xander jogging to catch up to her.

"Hey! Where's your bike?" Lucy called.

"I parked it at the school parking lot!" he called, catching up to her. He barely even panted to catch his breath, which implied he was in great shape. She liked guys in great shape. "If you won't let me drive you, I'll walk you home."

Lucy couldn't stop herself from grinning. That . . . was kind of adorable. "Okay, fine. If you insist."

With triumphant glee, Xander linked his arm through hers as the crosswalk light changed. They headed across the street.

"So, where should we go?" he asked casually.

"I assume my house, since you're walking me home."

"No, no, no, don't be boring. We should stop somewhere on the way. I know a great ice skating rink."

"That would make this a date, and this isn't a date."

"Who says?" Xander asked with a gleam in his eye.

"My dad," Lucy said dryly. "He forbade me to go out with you after how Alex described you, and he has to approve every one of my first dates before I'm allowed to go out with them. It's a drag, but I'm not breaking that rule, because I want to still be allowed to go out."

Xander looked a little sulky. "Well, we'll have to convince your dad I'm a prize specimen, then."

Not Quite Welcome

Lucy giggled at the petulance on his face. "First you'll have to convince me. I'm still not sure I trust you."

They were nearing Brudger's Ice Cream Heaven, where a lot of students hung out after school.

"Here!" Xander said, pointing. "How 'bout here?"

Lucy considered that for a moment. It was a possible date spot, but it was also a spot where you could just hang out with a friend. She'd been here quite a few times with Natasia, Jezza, Matilda, and Carrie. "Okay."

They went inside and waited at the end of a long line. The booths inside were pretty crowded, like they usually were after school.

Xander pulled out a coin and started to flip it.

"What're you doing?" Lucy asked curiously.

"Picking a flavor. I always pick randomly." He caught the coin and looked at it. "Tails. Okay, now for the next digit."

"Next digit?" Lucy repeated.

"Yep," Xander grinned. "There are sixteen flavors. Perfect for assigning them numbers in binary and flipping a coin to pick."

That sounded suspiciously like math, which Lucy wanted to have nothing to do with. She made a face.

"C'mon," he laughed. "It's way more fun than you'd think. Surprise is the spice that makes boring things delicious."

"Ice cream isn't boring," Lucy retorted.

"Ah, but it can always be *more* interesting." Xander tossed the coin in the air again. "Life's only an adventure when you make space for randomness."

He might have a point, Lucy admitted.

"Okay, pick randomly for me, too," she said impulsively.

Xander grinned. "I knew there was a reason I liked you."

Lucy's lighthearted mood vanished. "There is a reason, and it's not as innocent as love at first sight."

"Aw, c'mon!" Xander punched her in the arm. "I don't care, so why should you? As far as I'm concerned, if it got us together, it's a good thing."

"We're not 'together'!" Lucy insisted.

"Not yet, maybe." He smirked.

Lucy did her best to hide a smile. She didn't want to encourage his cockiness, but the fact that he was so sure of himself was fun. She felt like she didn't have to worry about bruising his ego, unlike some guys, who were super fragile.

Plus, it was really, really nice to meet a guy who knew about her power and even consented to it using itself on him. Sometimes it really bothered her that she never knew if a guy's feelings were real or fake. At least with Xander, it didn't matter, because it was the same to him either way.

"Hope you like pistachio with almond slivers," Xander said as they got to the register. "'Cause that's what you're getting."

"Fine, but only if you're paying. I have no idea if that'll be good or not."

"Twist my arm," Xander grinned, taking out his wallet.

Oh, wait! Lucy realized. *If he pays, that means this is a date!*

"Never mind," she said hastily, scrambling in her jeans pocket for her wallet. "I'll pay for my own —"

"No, no, no, no. You said it. You can't take it back," he said, swatting her wallet away.

"Well, it's still not a date!" Lucy protested.

The guy behind the cash register looked very amused as he swiped Xander's card.

Chapter 3
Not Quite a Date

Great the pistachio ice cream was not, but it wasn't half bad once she coated it in whipped cream and poured chocolate chips all over it.

"That's cheating," Xander opined.

"Well, then I'm glad I'm cheating," Lucy shot back.

Xander cackled.

"Easy for you!" she added. "You got butterscotch fudge ripple with cookie dough mix-ins!"

"Wanna try some?" he asked. And then, without waiting for her permission, he grabbed a spoonful and poked it in her mouth.

"Hey!" Lucy protested with her mouth full. She paused. "Wow, that's really good. But hey! Your germs are on that spoon!"

"You mean we've *shared germs?*" Xander asked with mock horror. "Guess it won't matter if I kiss you afterwards, then."

Lucy gave him a narrow-eyed glare. "Don't try it. I don't kiss on the first date."

"I thought you said this isn't a date."

"It isn't! I don't kiss guys I'm just hanging out with, either!"

"Guess I'll have to see if I can tempt you out of that policy." Xander's eyes were gleaming.

Lucy folded her arms. She wasn't sure yet if she really liked him or found him really exasperating.

"Tell you what," Xander said, leaning forward. "Let's go on a first date tonight."

"Can't," Lucy said. "I have a date with Ivan."

Xander's eyes looked suddenly dangerous. "Who's Ivan?"

"A guy at school," Lucy retorted. "You'd know that if you weren't a dropout."

Xander sat back, looking amused. "I'm not a dropout. I just go to a different school."

"Uh huh. Right."

"No, really. I can recite you the whole thing I had to memorize for English class last week. 'To be or not to be' —"

"I don't care," Lucy cut in. "Your life is your business. We're not dating, anyway."

"Wanna see the equations I memorized for Trigonometry?" Xander slid out of the booth, snatched the pen from the register, and grabbed a napkin from the dispenser. He started to scribble on it. "Here's the first one —"

"I wouldn't know the difference between a real and fake equation if it reached out and bit me," Lucy informed him.

Xander stared at her in confusion. "Aren't you in the same math class as Alex?"

"Yeah. I'm failing out of it," Lucy said sourly.

"Sounds like you need a math tutor."

"You volunteering?" she asked with interest. One of the guys she was currently dating, George, had started out as her math tutor last year.

Xander guffawed. "Not hardly! Sounds like the most boring date idea possible."

Lucy had to agree. Besides, she didn't totally believe he wasn't a dropout. It made no sense for him to go to a different school. Unless it was a private school, she supposed, but then why would he go and not Alex?

Not Quite a Date

"Why do you go to a different school?" she challenged.

"Because Alex doesn't like being around me," Xander said with a lazy smile. "He thinks I'm embarrassing."

"*Are* you embarrassing?"

"Only because it's really funny to embarrass him." Xander grinned.

Lucy put her hands on her hips. "You sound like a prize of a brother."

"Hey," Xander snapped, sitting forward. "When you've had a . . . condition for seventeen years, then you can judge people. It's not just him it's hard on, you know."

That's right. Lucy swallowed. *He's known for pretty much his whole life that he was Alex's heir. He's known his whole life that his brother would die before they're adults, and then he'd be the next to go.*

"I'm sorry," she said in a low voice. "I only got mine a few weeks ago. My parents explained about what would be coming when I was six. When did you find out?"

"I don't wanna talk about it," Xander said abruptly. "Let's talk about something more fun. When *are* you free for a first date?"

"Umm . . ." Lucy tried to remember. "I think I'm booked through next week, and I don't want to schedule anything further than that, because then I'd have to start keeping track, and that would be a pain."

"You're super busy, and you don't keep track?" Xander asked with a mocking smile.

"No, I don't!" Lucy snapped. "Being organized is one of the personality traits I'm trying to avoid!"

"Ah." The smile dropped from his face. "So you're trying to fight it."

"Of course I'm trying to fight it!" Lucy said indignantly. "What kind of person wouldn't?"

"You'd be surprised." Xander shrugged. "I've seen six different people die now, and not all of them made an effort to fight it. Two of them liked using their abilities so much that they succumbed within a few years."

Lucy was silent. She'd been so busy thinking that she had only twenty years left that she'd forgotten even that much time was an outlier.

"Aunt Aggie died after nine years," she said slowly. "What's the average?"

"She'd've lasted longer if she hadn't given up trying to fight it," Xander said. "It can be fast if the person doesn't try to fight it — maybe two or three years. For someone who does fight, fourteen or fifteen is more common. It depends a lot based on how close your natural personality is to . . . well, you know."

Lucy swallowed. She *did* know.

"Well, thankfully I'm almost the opposite!" she said, trying to look on the bright side. She was anything but the ideal Virgo.

"Yeah, but using what you can do makes the effect stronger," Xander said. "Those who never turn theirs off die faster. Enjoy being yourself while it lasts."

Lucy's breath caught in her throat. "That's so unfair! I *can't* turn mine off! I can't control it at all!"

"Yeah duh it's unfair. I don't make the rules."

Lucy squeezed her fists tightly. There were tears in her eyes.

"Hey. Hey." Xander slid out of his booth and sat next to her. He put his arm around her shoulders. "It stinks, I know. But I assumed you wanted the truth, not a pretty lie."

Lucy nodded, breathing shakily. Her eyes were blurry.

"Here." Xander reached out and grabbed a handful of napkins out of the dispenser on the table. "Blow your nose or something. Just don't wipe it on me. That would be gross."

Lucy giggled despite herself and took the napkins, blowing her nose loudly.

"Is there an elephant in here?" Xander looked around in mock bafflement.

"Shut up!" Lucy giggled through her tears and punched him in the shoulder.

Xander seemed to be debating saying something, and then finally spoke up.

"Look," he said reluctantly, "you can't have a boyfriend."

Not Quite a Date

Lucy looked up at him, confused.

Xander grimaced, looking like he was pulling teeth. "If you're naturally impulsive and flighty, and you've never dated anyone exclusively before . . . wanting a loyal relationship is probably what your ability is trying to push you into. If you give in to that . . . it'll make it easier to become stable and predictable in other areas of your life. Before you know it, you'll be different, and you won't even think that's a bad thing."

Lucy stared at him, astonished. "Is that why you think I have this . . . ability?" She couldn't say the words *magic* or *power.*

"Yeahhhhh . . ." Xander looked deeply disgruntled. "Based on what I've seen with others, I'm pretty sure it's something along those lines. It's certainly not trying to push you to enjoy having a dozen guys in love with you at all times. Most likely, it's trying to make you feel like that's a burden so that you'll want to settle down."

Lucy kissed him on the cheek. "You're an amazing person to tell me that."

"I wish I weren't," he grumbled.

"It shows that you really love me," she said, patting his cheek. "You don't want to see me die."

"Yeah, or I'm an idiot," he muttered. He glanced over, and a slight glint grew in his eye. "So, have I earned a real kiss?"

"No!" Lucy swatted his arm. "But you can walk me the rest of the way home."

Chapter 4
Not Quite as Fun

Her highly organized mother pestered her into doing all her math homework as soon as she got home, because apparently the math teacher had called her mom about the state of Lucy's test today. Joy.

She barely had enough time left to get dressed in a new outfit and spray on perfume in preparation for her date with Ivan.

"One good thing about Lucy going out every night is that it'll lower our food budget," she heard her mother teasing her father in the kitchen.

"I'd rather just pay for her food," he grumbled.

"This is a second date, Dad, so you've already met Ivan," Lucy said in a bossy voice as she strode into the kitchen. "There's no need to embarrass me by trying to approve him again."

"Who's Ivan?" he asked suspiciously. "I don't remember that name."

"Black curly hair, beautiful eyes?"

"Don't remember that at all."

"You made a really big deal about the nose ring?"

Not Quite as Fun

"Oh, yes." Her father glowered. "I didn't like him."

"You never like *any* of my dates, Dad."

"Well, maybe if you didn't go on quite so many of them —!"

Lucy's mom was snickering openly.

The doorbell rang, and Lucy ran to get it. Ivan, it seemed, was more punctual than she was. He was only five minutes late.

"Hi, Ivan!" she said cheerfully. She was startled when he shoved a dozen brightly colored flowers at her. "What are these?"

"Gerbera daisies," he said proudly. "They weren't cheap."

Okay? Lucy thought. She didn't care how much money a guy spent on her.

"Hey, Mom!" she called. "Can you come put these flowers in a vase?"

Her mother came to the front door. "Oh, lovely! I haven't seen gerbera daisies since the last time your father bought them for me!" She raised her voice in what was probably intended to be a subtle hint. "It's been a REALLY LONG TIME!"

"I bought you silk ones last time! They haven't wilted yet!" her father called back.

"Have fun, Lucy." Her mom kissed her on top of the head. "And Ivan, make sure you treat her well."

He drew himself up. "I have excellent plans," he said in a pompous voice. "She'll love them."

Lucy stared at him out of the corner of her eye. *Which means what?*

It turned out to mean La Belle Caille, a French restaurant that was the most expensive one in town. Lucy only knew that because her mother had begged her father to take her there for their anniversary, and he had looked up the prices of the menu online and screamed.

They'd eventually gone, but only because her mother had promised they could get pizza for their next anniversary.

Lucy felt more than a little out of her depth as a snooty waiter herded them into chairs by a table in a dim room that was mostly lit by candlelight. All the other people in the room were adults, and all of them were dressed really fancily.

"Um . . ." Lucy said awkwardly. "You know, Dave's Pizza Buffet would've been fine."

"Nonsense," Ivan said with a superior smile. "Any guy can take you there. Could any guy at school take you *here*?"

Do I want any guy at school to take me here? Lucy thought doubtfully, looking at the menu. It was entirely in French. There were illustrations for some of the meals, but not all of them, and in the dim lighting, she couldn't be one hundred percent sure that none of them were frog legs.

Or snails. Didn't French people eat snails? She didn't want to eat snails. Sweat prickled on the back of her neck just thinking about it.

She still hadn't decided what was safe enough to order by the time the waiter came. Ivan ordered what he wanted, rattling it off in what sounded like French and watching to see if Lucy was impressed.

Lucy was not impressed. It was probably his foreign language at school. She was taking Spanish, and could order just fine from the menu of a Mexican place, thank you.

"And for you, mademoiselle?" the waiter asked politely.

"Ummm . . ." Lucy scrutinized the menu. She was afraid to try any of the dinner options. "Do you have salad? With, like, chicken or bacon or something and no frog legs or anything?"

"Oui, mademoiselle. We have one that has both chicken and bacon. It also has tomatoes, croutons, and cheese. Our croutons are specially made, and they are magnificent."

"They're made out of bread, right?" she asked nervously.

"Yes." The waiter seemed to be trying to keep a straight face.

"And no frog legs? Or snails?" she asked anxiously.

"No, mademoiselle."

"Perfect," Lucy said with relief.

He made a note on his notepad. "What kind of salad dressing would you like?"

"Ranch."

"Very well, mademoiselle."

The waiter left.

Not Quite as Fun

Ivan's face was pinched as he looked at her. "You don't have to order the cheapest thing on the menu. I can afford better."

"I'm on a diet," Lucy improvised.

The I-don't-want-to-eat-frog-legs diet, she added silently.

Ivan looked disgruntled as he shook out his cloth napkin and placed it on his lap.

Lucy eyed the breadsticks on the table and wondered if they were safe to eat. Maybe she should ask the waiter if there were snails inside them when he came back. Just in case.

As they sat in awkward silence, her mind wandered to her not-a-date with Xander earlier. If he were here, he'd probably order something random off the menu and make her do it, too. Then she'd wind up eating frog legs for sure. But maybe they'd turn out to be not so bad. Or even if they were, he'd laugh his head off about the face she made eating them.

Lucy shook her head. *Keep your mind on the date you're on.*

Into the awkward silence, Ivan started talking.

And talking. And talking.

About himself. Without pausing to take a break.

"Uh huh," Lucy interjected every so often, nodding at the right places as she ripped apart the breadsticks to check them for snails and wished she could just go home. "Yeah, sure."

Such noncommittal replies seemed to be all the encouragement he needed to keep on going, and going, and going.

Lucy's mind wandered all over the place as she gave up on listening. Mostly it kept wandering over to Xander.

It had been so nice of him to tell her what he'd figured out about her power, especially when he clearly hadn't wanted to. Knowing that the curse was trying to make her want a steady boyfriend, and therefore it was something she shouldn't want, paradoxically made her really want one. She'd always assumed she would get one eventually; she'd just never been in a hurry.

And even the risk of shortening her lifespan had to be better than a hundred more dates like this.

Ivan was still talking. And talking. And talking. She wasn't even nodding and saying "uh huh" anymore.

Sheesh, could the guy take a hint?!

It felt like the date lasted forever, but it was really only about an hour. When Ivan finally took her home and walked her to the front door, she nearly breathed a sigh of relief.

Then he leaned forward and kissed her. Hard. With tongue.

Lucy shoved him away. "Goodnight, Ivan. I'll see you at school."

"When can we have our third date?"

"Never!" she shouted. "I didn't have fun! Take a hint!"

His face fell in devastation, and Lucy rapidly escaped inside, slamming the door. She was sorry to hurt his feelings, and she would've been nicer, but come on! What had he been thinking?!

"How was the date?" her dad asked, walking quickly from the kitchen, a mug of chamomile tea splashing on his hand. He was never far from the door when she was off on a date.

"Awful," Lucy snorted. "I'm never going out with him again."

"Really?" Her dad's face brightened. "I'm sorry to hear that!"

Lucy rolled her eyes. "You could try to be a teeny bit less transparent, Dad."

"I could try. I could definitely try." He beamed and kissed her on the head. "Goodnight, Lucy. Have sweet dreams."

"Goodnight, Dad. You can give the flowers to Mom if you want to. I don't mind."

"Great idea! She loves gerbera daisies."

"Cool. Then someone can get something fun out of that date." Lucy headed up to her room, in a rather sour mood.

Her father skipped up the stairs to bed, whistling cheerfully.

Chapter 5
Not Quite the Plan

Natasia and Sean had plans the next day, Matilda and Jezza were working on a group project they were doing for art class, and Carrie had a first date with her newest "boyfriend," who apparently was not the guy who worked at the mall, but one of the guys on the basketball team.

So Lucy was, again, left to walk home alone.

Not so alone, though. Because Xander was already waiting outside the school building, helmet under his arm.

"Do you know me enough to ride with me now?" he asked.

"No," Lucy said with a teasing grin. "But I don't mind walking with you again."

"Okay." He zipped the helmet into a bag at the side of his motorcycle. "What if we made a detour to Dave's Pizza Buffet this time?"

"It's not on the way to my house."

"But it *is* in walking distance from the school."

Lucy snorted with laughter. "All right. But it's still not a date, you know. We're just hanging out."

"Whatever you want to call it," he said grandly.

As they walked across the school grounds to reach the exit on the other end, a dozen jealous boys eyed them with angry eyes.

With a glint in his eye, Xander took Lucy's hand and kissed it flamboyantly.

"Xander!" Lucy exclaimed, snatching her hand away.

"I'm not allowed to show my affection?" he asked innocently.

"Not when you're clearly just trying to make them jealous!"

"I'm not trying to make them jealous." Xander smirked. "I'm trying to show them that they haven't got a chance because you belong to me."

"If you act like a dog and try to mark your turf, I'm going to slap you," Lucy said darkly.

Xander guffawed. "So much for my clever plan!"

When they arrived at Dave's Pizza Buffet, Lucy was appalled to notice that five different guys from school had followed them here and were waiting in line behind them.

"I know it isn't safe for you to date one guy exclusively, but I recommend not taking dates from guys who act like stalkers," Xander said casually, indicating the crowd behind them with his head.

"Yes, thank you, that same thought's occurred to me," Lucy said tightly.

She glanced back and stared surreptitiously at the five guys, one at a time, looking for a reason to find each one unattractive. Darian had a mole on his ear — she'd never noticed that before. Dale had a single hair growing out of his left eyebrow that was almost an inch long. Adrian's neck was way longer than usual. Stewart had grubby fingernails. Eddie, well, he was perfect, but the fact that he had followed her here was enough to make her feel like he was kind of creepy.

There, Lucy thought, turning around. *I hope that's enough.*

Her power could be a bummer sometimes, but at least it *did* stop working on the guys she stopped finding attractive. That was very helpful. It was also one of the reasons she felt no guilt about squashing Ivan's heart yesterday. He'd recover fast.

Unless, of course, his feelings were real, which was certainly possible. But she hoped not. She hoped the only guy who ever had real feelings for her would be the one she'd choose to be a permanent boyfriend.

Permanent? Lucy thought, smacking the side of her head. *You know you can't do that. It'll make you die sooner and lose who you are faster. Stop thinking about that!*

They reached the front of the line, and Xander paid for both of them before she could stop him.

"Hey!" Lucy objected, waving her wallet.

"Oops, I forgot," Xander said innocently, not looking sorry at all.

They loaded up their plates with various slices of pizza, and Lucy checked the entrance. To her relief, two of her five followers had left, and the other three looked like they were rethinking why they were here.

"So, let's see if I can find some good first date questions . . ." Xander said, pulling up the browser on his phone.

"This isn't a date!" Lucy repeated.

"Here's a good one," Xander said with a grin. "What was your favorite Disney movie as a child?"

"This *still* isn't a date," Lucy informed him.

"Okay, I'll take a guess." Xander grinned and put his chin in his hand. "I bet it was . . . hmmm . . . *Beauty and the Beast.*"

"What? No!" Lucy exclaimed. "It was *The Little Mermaid!* Belle's okay, I guess, but she is way too obsessed with books. And the talking plates creeped me out."

"Really?" Xander raised his eyebrows teasingly. "You prefer the girl who chases after a stranger like some clueless stalker?"

"For your information, Prince Eric is *cute!*" Lucy swatted him in the arm. "Any girl would fall in love with him at first sight! You can tell he's really nice, and he's got dimples, and —"

"Uh huh," Xander said, grinning.

"Anyway, she's not the best part of the movie," Lucy defended. "King Triton is."

Xander stared at her. "The overprotective dad?"

"Yes!" Lucy exclaimed, putting her hands to her chest. "Oh, my gosh, he's so sweet! He loves his daughter so much, and he'd do anything for her, and then he *does*, and oh, my gosh!"

". . . Right," Xander said, looking baffled. "If you say so."

"Well, what was your favorite?" Lucy asked, picking up one of her slices of pizza. "Wait, let me guess — it was *Robin Hood*."

"Nah, too much romance," Xander said. "It was *The Sword in the Stone*."

"Really?" Lucy wrinkled her nose. She'd only seen that movie once, and hadn't thought much of it. "I wouldn't have guessed you were the knight in shining armor type."

"Are you kidding?" Xander exclaimed. "I love King Arthur! Chivalry and all that stuff — it's awesome! Half the reason I bought a motorbike in the first place is because it's as close as you can get to being a modern-day knight."

"Seriously?"

"Seriously!"

"Wow, you are weird."

"Says the girl who likes the overprotective dad character."

"He's *sweet!*" Lucy cried.

They finished off their pizza slices, bantering and laughing together, and then headed out of the pizza buffet and towards her house.

When they got there, Xander impulsively grabbed her hand and kissed it.

Lucy giggled, opened the door, and darted into the house without saying goodbye.

Unfortunately, her dad was home and standing right there.

"Who was that?!" he roared.

"Alex's brother Xander," Lucy said, deciding that telling the truth was the best option.

"The Gemini's heir?!"

"Well-remembered."

"You can't date the Gemini's heir!" he exploded. "Your mother was born in the Gemini dates! If you married him and had a kid who was Gemini, she'd be the next to inherit that curse!"

Not Quite the Plan

"I never said I was going to marry him!" Lucy defended. "I'm not even dating him! I'd've brought him to meet you if I was! Sheesh!"

"I just saw him kiss you!"

"On the *hand!* I'll kiss you, too!" Lucy pecked her dad on the cheek. "See?"

"It looked very different from what I was seeing," he glowered.

"That's because you're King Triton."

He looked baffled. "Who?"

"Never mind." Her lips twitched. "I love you, Dad, and I'm going upstairs. Stop worrying about me."

She ran up the stairs to her room two at a time, tossed her backpack on the floor, and glanced in the mirror to notice her hair was a mess. She grabbed the hairbrush from her dresser and started to brush through her hair, humming. Since she had *The Little Mermaid* on her mind, it reminded her of a scene where Ariel did the same thing —

Oh, no. Lucy put the hairbrush on her dresser and looked in the mirror.

She was falling in love with Xander, wasn't she?

Darn it! This was not the plan! she thought fiercely.

Chapter 6
Not Quite Relaxed

Obviously going on another not-a-date with Xander was out of the question, so Lucy threw herself into all of her other dates that week, and asked various guys at school to drive her home on the days her friends weren't available to hang out with. A lot of them jumped at the chance.

Meanwhile, she had the fun ordeal of three first dates for three nights in a row. One of them went well enough that she agreed to give him a second date sometime. The other two resulted in her politely dodging the question and looking for a reason to find the guy unattractive, hoping he wouldn't ask her again.

So she was rather looking forward to Saturday, when she had a fourth date with a guy she knew she liked quite a lot.

Unfortunately, that date wound up the most awkward of them all.

"So," Pablo said when he picked her up in his car, "you know how your dad, um, wanted to meet me on our first date?"

"Yep," Lucy said, nodding. "He insists on embarrassing me."

"Well . . ." Pablo wriggled. "Guess what."

Not Quite Relaxed

"Your father wants to meet me?" Lucy guessed.

"And my mother, and my uncles, and my aunts, and my sisters, and my grandmother." Pablo laughed awkwardly.

"That sounds like . . . a lot of people," Lucy said slowly.

"I know." Pablo clunked his head against the steering wheel. "I've told them not to bother you, but all my relatives showed up an hour before I was supposed to leave to get you and said that they wouldn't let me back in the house until they met you."

"Wow." Lucy was taken aback. "They're pretty hardcore."

"You don't have to go," Pablo said quickly. "I mean . . . they might drive all over town looking for us if we don't, but . . . we can *try* to hide from them if you want!"

It almost seemed like he thought that was the better option.

Lucy snorted with laughter. "They're really serious about this, aren't they?"

"They make your dad look like a softie," Pablo groaned.

"Wow." By this point, Lucy was more curious than intimidated. They couldn't possibly be as bad as he was making them out to be. "Sure, I'll meet them. Why not?"

"You might find out why not," Pablo said darkly, turning the key to start the car. "My relatives would try the patience of a saint."

"Well, sainthood is something no one's ever accused me of before!" Lucy said with a laugh. Seriously, at this point, she was burning with curiosity to meet these people. Could they really be as bad as he said?

♍

As it turned out . . . yes.

Yes, they could.

"LUCY!" A plump Hispanic woman greeted her at the door as soon as Pablo rang the doorbell. She proceeded to chatter in a high-pitched, excited voice. "I'm so pleased to meet you! Pablo, she's so pretty! And you two look so good together! Imagine how cute your kids will be!"

"Uh . . ." Lucy said, a little slack-jawed.

"Mom . . ." Pablo said, with a hand over his eyes.

"Come in! Come in!" the woman cried, gesticulating wildly for them to come inside.

They were ushered into a room crammed with people and a clamor of voices. And crucifixes. Lots of crucifixes. More crucifixes than people. She wasn't sure which was more intimidating.

"Is that her?!"

"Hey, she's prettier than Pablo deserves!"

"Aw, my little nephew's so grown-up! He's finally bringing a girl home!"

Lucy glanced over at Pablo, overwhelmed at their excitement. He was hanging his head and looking like he wanted to die.

"H-hi," Lucy said, waving sheepishly. "I'm Lucy Martin. Nice to meet you all."

"Have a seat, have a seat!" A man who had to be either Pablo's father or one of his uncles grabbed Lucy's hand and pulled her to a chair that was within easy view of everyone else.

With a sense of impending doom, Lucy sat in it.

The flood of questions began.

"You *are* Catholic, right?" an old woman who had to be Pablo's grandmother demanded.

"Y-yesssss?" Lucy said hesitantly. She'd never gone to mass for any other reason than Christmas or Easter, but technically yes.

"How long have you and Pablo been dating?"

"This is our fourth date —"

"Are you serious about him? Are you going to marry him?" either a cousin or a younger sister giggled.

"Um, it's way too early to say —"

"Do you have a middle name? Pablo's never told us."

"It's Jennifer —"

"Do you have brothers and sisters?"

"A sister. She's in college right —"

"Have you and Pablo talked about the number of children you'd like to have yet?" a father or uncle asked briskly.

"Um?!"

"I think you should get married in June!" declared a cousin or a younger sister.

Not Quite Relaxed

"Like I said," Lucy said, beginning to feel slightly panicked, "it's way too early to —"

"And if I'm going to be a bridesmaid, I want a pink dress, not a yellow one. Yellow makes me look fat. I'm just saying."

Lucy kept a desperately fixed smile on her face and tried to answer the questions that were lobbed at her at a dizzying speed.

After half an hour of really personal questions, culminating in an unbelievable one from an aunt about whether infertility ran in her family or whether she personally had any "period issues" that could potentially cause it, Pablo leapt up and said:

"Oh, look! We have to leave right now to make our dinner reservation in time! Come on, Lucy!"

Before anyone could react, he seized Lucy's hand, tugged her up to her feet, and fled for the door with her in tow.

Of course, half of his relatives leapt out of their seats and chased after them, but Pablo and Lucy were faster.

He must have left the doors unlocked, because he had the passenger's side open for Lucy in a flash, and then was in the driver's side before the first of the sisters-or-cousins reached the car and banged on the window.

"Sorry! Gonna be late!" Pablo called, turning his key in the ignition.

Lucy was panting for breath and giggling uncontrollably as she tried to buckle her seat belt while they screeched around the corner to escape the crowd of younger-sisters-or-cousins yelling after them. "Do we really have dinner reservations?"

"Yup," Pablo said, his eyes glued to the road as he drove thirty miles over the speed limit. "I specifically called Dave's Pizza Buffet and told them to expect us at five o'clock so that we'd have an excuse to get out of there."

Lucy was giddy. "You know they don't reserve tables, right?"

"It's amazing how much I don't care!"

They screeched around another corner, and then finally slowed to the speed limit once they were well out of sight of the house.

"So . . . when you said they were worse than my dad, I thought you meant they *wouldn't* like me," Lucy commented.

"Oh, no, they like you. You're the first girl I've ever dated more than one time," Pablo said in an exasperated tone. "Naturally, they think that means they can assume wedding bells."

Lucy started giggling uncontrollably. Now that they were away from his relatives, their extreme nosiness seemed hilarious. "Are you the only person they've done that to?"

"Ha!" said Pablo. "No! You should've seen them when my cousin Teresa got engaged!"

"I think I'd like to hear the story," Lucy said with a grin.

"Oh, it's a long and terrible tale," Pablo intoned. "It all began when she showed up at the door with a boyfriend she hadn't told anybody she was dating, which was probably a wise move on her part . . ."

"Hang on," Lucy said, holding up her finger. "First, um, I just have to ask. Why all the crucifixes?"

"Huh?" Pablo glanced over at her, looking mystified. Then his face cleared. "Ohhhh! My mom collects those. Would you have preferred to have been in the living room? That's where she keeps her antique teapots."

Crucifixes versus fragile antiques that could easily break? That took less than a second of thought. "Nope, I definitely preferred the crucifixes."

"Yeah, me too. I wish she'd get a display cabinet instead of keeping those teapots on the tables. It makes the living room impossible to sit in comfortably."

Lucy suddenly started to giggle, imagining what would happen if she and Pablo did someday get married, and her father met Pablo's family in a living room full of fragile antiques strewn every which way. It'd be hard to tell what part of the situation would panic him more.

"What's so funny?" Pablo asked curiously.

"Nothing." Lucy straightened her face. "So, tell the story!"

Thankfully, Pablo wasn't nosy. "Okay. So, my cousin Teresa showed up out of the blue one day . . ."

Chapter 7
Not Quite Alone

By the time Tuesday rolled around, Lucy was doing quite a good job of not thinking about Xander.

Matilda and Jezza invited her to go to the mall with them on Monday, her first date with Billy that evening was fun, her father only *slightly* humiliated her during his usual intimidation of a new guy, she was back to completely ignoring her math homework, and overall, things were going well.

Until Xander showed up in the middle of her sixth date with George.

They were waiting in line at the movie theater, negotiating about which of the not-very-interesting movies looked less snooze-worthy than others, when Xander sauntered over with a leather jacket slung over his shoulder.

"There you are!" he called. "Have you been avoiding me?"

Lucy tensed and looked at George.

He gave her a questioning look.

She nodded.

"Nah, she's fine!" George called. "Want to join us?"

Lucy stared at him in horror. *I meant yes, please get rid of him, not yes, invite him along on our date!*

But it was too late. Xander was already joining them.

"What're the options?" he asked, craning his neck to look at the ticket window.

"Nothing great," George said. "But I saw the trailer for that one with the explosions, and it looked pretty good. Lucy thinks the romance looks more interesting, though."

Xander surveyed the posters on the wall beside them. The line moved forward as someone at the front chose their tickets and went into the theater. "Let's go to the romance," he said. "Then Lucy gets what she wants."

George grinned crookedly. "Good point. I assume you've got a thing for her, too?"

"Yeah, obviously," Xander smirked.

Lucy stared at her date in exasperation. George was one of the least jealous guys in existence. It was something she'd always liked about him, but did he have to be this comfortable about sharing her right now?

She wound up sandwiched between the two guys to watch a soppy romance movie, with a giant tub of popcorn parked on her lap that the two had agreed to split the cost of. Both of them casually reached out and took her hand that was near them, which meant she had no hands to grab popcorn to eat herself.

This, Lucy thought sourly, *is completely ridiculous.*

The forgettable movie plot ended eventually with a kiss in the rain at the sunset, and then the three of them headed out of the theater, the two boys chatting like old friends about a basketball game they'd seen on TV.

"I've seen you around at school," George said. "Aren't you on the basketball team?"

"Nah, that's Alex. We're twins. I go to a different school. I'm not on any teams, but I'm better at sports than he is. Try getting him to admit that, though." Xander grinned.

"Xander," Lucy interrupted, "I hope you realize this is my date with George."

Not Quite Alone

"Yeah, true. Thanks for letting me cut in, dude," Xander said.

"No problem." George gave him a thumbs-up. "I know Lucy likes having as many guys around as possible, and I want her to have a good time."

Lucy stopped and gave him an aggrieved look. He didn't seem to notice.

They reached the spot in the parking lot with George's car, and he unlocked the driver's side door.

"Hey, you got a ride home?" he asked Xander.

"Nah, Alex dropped me off when I saw Lucy standing in line," Xander said. "I can call him to get me."

"Eh, won't be necessary." George unlocked the back. "Just tell me where your house is, and I'll take you there before I take Lucy home."

Lucy let out a loud sigh. She'd always liked how casual and low-pressure George was, but really? Now he was treating their third wheel like an old friend? Really?

Xander glanced at her and caught the look on her face. He raised his eyebrows with a mischievous smirk and said, "Sure. That'd be great."

His "house" turned out to be a run-down apartment building with his motorcycle parked right by a dumpster. Through the window, Lucy could see Alex sitting on a worn out sofa, flipping the page of a book.

"Thanks, man," Xander said, getting out of the car. "Hey, do you mind if I ask Lucy something in private before I go?"

George laughed. "If it's a date, I think she's already booked through next week."

"Nah, it's about something else. It'll only take a second. Is that okay?"

"Sure," George said, shrugging.

Lucy rolled her eyes heavenward and got out of the car, following Xander across the parking lot so that they were out of earshot. She folded her arms. "What?"

"Just want to point out that you should hang on to him," Xander said. "He's a good choice."

Lucy blinked. That wasn't what she'd expected. "What?"

"Dude seems incapable of jealousy," Xander said. "I could tell you were annoyed about that, but you shouldn't be. That's just what you need: at least two guys who don't get jealous. You could dump all the rest and still be pretty safe."

Lucy's stomach flipped over.

"Are you saying you're the other one?" she challenged.

"I wouldn't say I'm *incapable* of jealousy, but . . . yeah, I can handle it." Xander grinned. "Especially since I know why you can't choose only one. And I don't mind him."

"Thank you so much for having opinions about my love life," Lucy snorted. "Maybe you could try not horning in on my dates in the future?"

"I'll do it if you'll give me a real first date."

"My dad would kill me. No!"

"Aw, c'mon." Xander grinned. "What's he got against me?"

"How about the thing your brother has that you're going to get eventually? The one that could endanger my whole family?"

A wall of fury slammed over Xander's eyes. Lucy swallowed involuntarily.

Then it was gone.

"Well," he said easily, "the only danger there is if we plan to have kids eventually. Even if one thing did lead to another and we wanted to get married — which is way off my radar right now! — I could always get a vasectomy or something. Problem solved."

Lucy stared at him. That was a possibility she hadn't considered.

"So?" Xander said. "You bring me to meet your dad, and I'll tell him that I'll do that if we want to get serious. Agreed?"

Lucy hesitated. It would certainly be interesting to see how her father would respond to that line of reasoning and if he'd be left speechless. But she had another concern right now. That flash of anger . . . that had freaked her out.

"I'll think about it," she said. "Let me think about it. Okay?"

"Okay." He swept into a grand bow and grabbed her hand and kissed it. "Whatever you wish, my lady."

She giggled in surprise.

Not Quite Alone

Watching him saunter to his front door, looking pleased with himself, Lucy's heart fluttered. He was sure cute. And she loved a whimsical romantic gesture.

How could she *not* fall for someone who did something like that so naturally?

But . . . but maybe there was another side to him that he wasn't showing her.

Maybe he was dangerous.

Swallowing and trying not to look unsettled, Lucy headed back to the car where George was waiting.

"What'd he want to ask you?" he asked as Lucy got in.

"Oh, if I wanted to go on a double date with him and Alex," Lucy lied, shrugging. "I told him maybe, but only if Alex picks a girl who isn't as boring as he is. That guy has no personality, seriously."

George chuckled as he backed out of the parking lot.

Chapter 8
Not Quite the Truth

"Um, where exactly do you think you're going?" Lucy's dad asked as she walked past him down the stairs to grab her coat from the rack.

"Out with Carrie," Lucy said.

For some reason, she hadn't scheduled a date for tonight, which meant she had a whole evening free, which meant that she could spend it reconnecting with her oldest friend and hopefully salvaging a friendship that had become decidedly rocky since she'd gotten the curse.

"No, you're not," her father said.

"Dad," Lucy said with exasperation, zipping up her coat, "I'm done with my homework. It's five. I'll be back by curfew."

"Well, then the people who are coming here specifically to see you will be very surprised to find you not here."

Lucy paused, and groaned. She'd completely forgotten that her mother had called for a meeting of all the other cursed. She wanted their advice of what precise things she should be tracking in Lucy's behavior to watch for how the curse was affecting her.

Not Quite the Truth

"Do I have to?" Lucy hedged. "They're coming to talk to Mom, not me. And I hate that color-coded spreadsheet."

"Let's see," Lucy's father said, rubbing his chin thoughtfully. "Allow my daughter to skip out of a commitment she's made, or hold her to not being rude to a bunch of people who are taking time out of their lives to come help her out. Let's see. Tough decision . . ."

"All right, all right," Lucy said grumpily, unzipping her coat. "But Carrie's going to jump to the worst possible conclusion if I call her to cancel now. She's going to think I got a last-minute date and just ditched her or something."

"Well, I'm sure she'll forgive you," her dad said, folding his thick, muscular arms as he stood in front of the door.

Lucy snorted loudly. Maybe that rock-hard face impressed the soldiers he trained down at the base, but she was too used to her dad to be cowed. Instead, she stomped up the stairs to her room, trying to think of some way to tell Carrie that she was not, in fact, on her way without explaining the complicated reason.

Bad news. Dad says I can't go, she texted finally.

Jerk! Carrie responded. *What's his damage?*

He's being MY DAD.

Ugh! I hate him! Carrie shot back.

Lucy winced. She didn't want to see Carrie insulting her dad, especially when he was a great guy most of the time. But there wasn't really any other way to stop Carrie from getting mad at her than to use her father as an excuse.

Sorry, Lucy said. *I've gotta work on stuff now. I hate math homework, yuck!*

Then she turned off the screen of her phone and tossed it on her bed, flopping back and putting her arm over her eyes.

Lucy sighed loudly. It really stank to be cursed. Now she was lying to her friends?

Maybe she should check her math homework again just so that she wouldn't have been lying to Carrie. She got out of bed, fetched her backpack, and pulled out the textbook and binder with her homework paper.

She found something she'd gotten wrong, and erased it and redid the problem. She saw another mistake and fixed that, too. Hey, this was actually starting to make sense for once in her life! It was almost like she was seeing things in a brand new way —

Lucy stopped abruptly, her pencil hovering over the paper. She reached out for her phone and pulled up a browser. When Google came up, she typed in, *Are Virgos good at math?*

Why yes, Google informed her, they were known for that!

Lucy snarled and slammed her phone onto her bedspread.

So now she had to be suspicious if she ever started to get better at school. Great. That was just great.

"Lucy!" her mother's voice called from downstairs. "Aaron and Catherine are here!"

Who's Catherine? Lucy wondered.

That turned out to be the Leo, she discovered after she went downstairs. She hadn't met the woman at the previous meeting because she was a high-powered executive who was usually busy at work, but she'd managed to come today.

Catherine and her mother hit it off way too well, and they immediately sat down at the kitchen table with the color-coded spreadsheet to talk about about its columns or something.

"Hi, Aaron," Lucy said, waving at the brown-skinned old man who had come with Catherine. She'd met him at the last meeting. He was the Aries. "How are things?"

"The usual," he said with a wry smile. "Stiff. Sore. I can't recommend old age."

"Well, I won't have to worry about that," Lucy said flippantly.

Aaron's smile suddenly looked very awkward.

"No big deal. I've gotten used to it." Lucy waved her hand. "Mom made cookies. Do you like cookies?"

"I love them, but unfortunately, I have to watch what I eat." He looked a bit embarrassed.

"Okay. No biggie." Lucy tried to think of a subject that would be less awkward. It was hard to know how to talk to an old person you weren't related to. With a grandparent, you could always ask for embarrassing stories about your parents when they were kids.

Not Quite the Truth

Fortunately, the doorbell rang again.

"I'll get it!" Lucy yelled, running for the front door.

She opened it to see both Alex and Xander.

"Hello, Lucy," Alex said quietly, raising a hand in greeting.

"Hi, Alex," Lucy said, barely glancing at him. "And Xander! What're you doing here?"

"This meeting's about you, right?" he said with a teasing grin. "Wouldn't miss it."

"You had better not try to flirt with me in front of my dad," she warned. "He'll blow up."

"I can exercise self-control," he said, his eyes glittering.

She stepped aside to let them into the house. Alex walked over to Aaron and the two got into what seemed to be an engrossing conversation, no doubt about something abundantly boring.

Spying Xander, Lucy's father detached himself from the conversation with his wife and Catherine about spreadsheets, which he didn't seem to find nearly as interesting as they did, and made a beeline for the guy.

"You're the Gemini's heir, right?" her dad demanded.

"Only on Tuesdays," Xander said glibly.

"What's that supposed to mean?" Lucy's dad growled.

"It means I'm being sarcastic, Pops. Lighten up."

Lucy groaned quietly.

"You," Lucy's father said to his daughter, pointing fiercely at Xander, "are not dating that boy!"

"I'm *not*, Dad! Sheesh, I told you already!"

"I'm sure we'll correct that eventually, though," Xander said cheerfully, plopping his arm around her shoulders.

Her father's face turned several colors at once.

"Xander!" Lucy exclaimed. "Alex, stop them!"

Alex glanced over, taking in the scene of his brother and her father engaged in a lock-eyed staring contest. Looking faintly amused, he just shook his head and turned away.

"Maybe I should give you 'the talk' now," Lucy's dad snarled, his face mottled red.

"Maybe you should," Xander agreed.

"But I have *no* intention of letting my daughter date you!"

"So she's told me," Xander said jauntily. He let go of Lucy's shoulders and blew her a kiss. "See you in a minute, sweet lips."

Then he sauntered off with her father into the living room.

Lucy stormed over to Alex, interrupting his conversation with Aaron. "Your brother," she announced, "is the most annoying person in the world!"

Aaron's lips quirked as he looked at Alex. "Would you agree with that assessment?"

Alex shrugged slightly, looking a bit embarrassed. "I would even say it's not news."

Gah! Why was Alex always so . . . so *calm* about everything? Was it that stupid Gemini curse he had? It had to be. He'd been the Gemini for seventeen years. By now, pretty much his whole personality had to be determined by the curse.

Lucy pulled her phone out of her jeans pocket and walked off to the corner of the hallway, looking up what the personality traits of Gemini were. Were they as mind-numbingly dull as Virgo's?

She stopped, and stared. She read the Google results, and then read them again.

"Adaptable. Outgoing. Indecisive. Impulsive. Loves being the center of attention. Huge flirt. Impulsive and unreliable."

But . . . but . . . that makes no sense! That doesn't describe Alex at all! In fact, it almost perfectly describes . . .

Lucy's heart caught in her throat.

. . . Xander.

Chapter 9

Not Quite the Heir

Xander was still in the living room with her father, which meant he wasn't available to confront. So Lucy stormed back to the kitchen and grabbed the next best thing.

"Alex," she snarled, seizing his arm, "can I talk to you for a minute?"

The guy raised his eyebrows. "Can it wait until you're not interrupting the conversation I'm in the middle of right now?"

"No," Lucy snapped.

Alex looked over at Aaron.

"Go ahead," the old man said graciously. "We can continue our conversation later."

Lucy dragged Alex upstairs, out of earshot of everyone else. She yanked her phone out of her pocket and shoved the screen with the description of Gemini in his face.

Alex just stared at her unblinkingly.

"Look!" Lucy snarled, pointing at the screen.

"Am I supposed to know what you're trying to communicate?" he queried.

"You're a big — fat — liar!" Lucy snarled, pulling her phone away and jabbing his chest with each word. "You're not the one who's affected! *Xander* is!"

"Oh," Alex said. "You noticed."

Lucy was stunned for a moment. He'd admitted it that readily?

"How could I not notice?!" she demanded.

"You'd be surprised," Alex said calmly. "Aaron knows, and so do my mom and my aunt and uncle, but I don't think anyone else has figured it out. Of course, there aren't that many people who know about the curses in the first place."

Lucy sucked in her breath. He had said "the curses." That proved for certain that he wasn't the Gemini. He wouldn't have been able to say that if he were.

"Well, if that's all . . ." Alex tried to head back downstairs.

"No, that isn't all!" Lucy sputtered, blocking his path. "Why would you lie about who has it?!"

Alex looked puzzled. "Does it make any difference?"

"YES!"

"Oh. Why?"

"Because!" Lucy exclaimed.

"Because . . .?"

Apparently she was going to have to spell it out.

"Because I have feelings for Xander, you moron," she said heatedly. "And apparently he's on the verge of dying!"

"And you prefer for me to be the one on the verge of dying," Alex said dryly.

"I didn't say that!"

"Oh, my mistake, I thought you just did."

"Fine," Lucy said with annoyance. "I'd prefer it to be you because I like Xander better. Happy?"

"Not really, although I might feel better about it if you would turn off your power, which is, by the way, still affecting me."

"Don't change the subject!" Lucy glared at him.

"It's not an unreasonable request, Lucy."

"Fine," Lucy snapped. "Then you can tell me why you think it's okay to lie about something so important."

Not Quite the Heir

She closed her eyes and focused on how irritating she found Alex when he wasn't boring, which was completely different from Xander, who was irritating-but-exciting. Being irritated by Xander was annoying in a fun way, like being teased by a friend about something embarrassing. Being irritated by Alex was just annoying.

"Better?" Lucy asked, opening her eyes.

Alex shrugged. "I hope so, but I won't be able to tell until you remove it from Xander, too. I can read his mind, remember."

"Well, that's too bad for you," Lucy said, putting her hands on her hips. "If he wants me to take it off him, he can tell me himself. I'm not even sure I can, because he's super my type. He might even be my favorite guy I'm currently dating!"

"You're not dating him," Alex said with an edge in his voice.

"Dad's giving him 'the talk' right now," Lucy retorted. "If he can convince Dad, I soon will be."

Alex looked decidedly sour-faced.

"Hang on!" Lucy exclaimed suddenly. "You enormous liar! You *can't* know what he's thinking! He's the one who's affected, so his ability wouldn't work on *you!*"

"It's two-way, Lucy," Alex said with a tight jaw. "It works on us equally."

Oh. Lucy stared at him with wide eyes. *Ohhhh!*

That explained a few things.

It explained why Xander had known all that homework stuff he'd brought up, even though he probably was a dropout and didn't go to school.

It explained how Alex could pretend he was the cursed one, if he really did have access to the power he claimed to have.

It even explained why Alex seemed to think it didn't matter which one was cursed, even though it mattered a *lot.*

"Well, fine," Lucy said. "Now explain to me why you've lied about the rest!"

"I've never lied," Alex said coolly. "I just haven't corrected the assumptions other people have made when I figured the details were none of their business in the first place."

"None of their . . .?" Lucy stared at him, aghast.

"Yes," Alex said in a chilly tone. "I know it might be an alien concept, but not everybody likes to gossip about their private life with every stranger they meet."

Boy, did she dislike him.

"Then why doesn't Xander tell anyone?" Lucy challenged. "Is he as unreasonably obsessed with privacy as you are?"

Alex set his jaw. "First of all, it's not unreasonable, and second, he *can't* tell people the details. Or have you forgotten how all of the curses work?"

Lucy stamped her foot. "Still! He could say it indirectly!"

"Why would he want to?" Alex shot back. "Do you think it's fun to have people pressuring you and wanting to know your mental state for every second out of the day?"

Lucy went silent. That was exactly what she'd been dodging from her mother ever since the curse had hit.

"So . . . you're taking it for him so that he doesn't have to?" Lucy said slowly. A realization occurred to her. "Because you feel you owe him? Because he's the one who's going to die first?"

Alex said nothing. His eyes were veiled.

Lucy sighed in exasperation. The way he so often went quiet was *so* annoying.

"Okay, I get it," she said. "You don't want to talk about it."

"Thank you."

"Just one more thing, though —"

"I take back my thank you."

"What was he *like?*" Lucy forged on, determined to get the answer. "What did he used to be like as a kid?"

Alex was silent.

"It's important!" Lucy cried.

"Why?" Alex's voice was very quiet. "It's a permanent change. It's not like he's going to revert."

"Because —" Lucy's voice cracked a little. She swallowed quickly and continued, trying to keep her voice level. "Because if I fell in love with somebody, I'd want him to love *Lucy*, not somebody else inhabiting my body. I'm guessing Xander feels the same way."

Not Quite the Heir

Alex looked at the floor and didn't speak.

"So what was he like as a kid?" Lucy asked urgently. "It's the closest I can get to knowing who he would be now without being changed against his will. I need to know, Alex. Please!"

Slowly, Alex looked up. His eyes were filled with pain. When he spoke, it was barely audible.

"He was pretty much exactly like me."

Then he shoved past her and went down the stairs.

Chapter 10
Not Quite a Choice

Reeling from the news, it was Lucy's turn to be dead silent, standing at the stop of the stairs as Alex reached the bottom and disappeared from view.

Xander was like Alex? Xander was like Alex?!

It wasn't good news. It was, in fact, the worst possible news.

If she had gotten any other answer, she may have been able to convince herself that she could have fallen for Xander without him being cursed.

But she *knew* Alex, and she knew she didn't like him.

Well, she liked his face, because who wouldn't? But that wasn't enough to really mean anything.

Pablo, and George, and Jonas, and Donny . . . all of them were great, all guys that she was happy to go out with.

But Xander was special. Xander knew about her curse, and didn't mind it. Xander had, in fact, told her it was fine to use her power on him. With every other guy, there was the uncomfortable question of whether he'd choose to date her without the power. With Xander . . . it didn't matter.

But it seemed she didn't actually have feelings for Xander. She had feelings for Gemini.

And she'd hate it if somebody fell in love with Virgo, instead of Lucy.

Which means I have to stop it, Lucy thought, clenching her fists so hard that her fingernails bit into her palms. *If I'd hate someone doing that to me, I can't do it to somebody else. It's wrong.*

She had to stop liking Xander. She had to stop finding him appealing. She had to make sure her power stopped working on him, so that he could run away to protect himself.

Because he surely wouldn't like her if she gave him a choice. He must have overheard her conversation with Alex. He knew she didn't love him; she loved Gemini. And unless he was suicidal, the last thing he ought to want was to hang out with a girl who was the perfect match for his curse. If he did, he'd fall into Gemini faster and faster, and die sooner.

Lucy closed her eyes and tried to think of things that were unappealing about Xander.

It was an uphill battle. Every time she thought of something she didn't like, such as the fact that she was pretty sure he was a dropout, one of those cocky grins or flamboyant hand-kisses sprang to her mind to drown it out.

But at last, she figured out something that she was absolutely sure she didn't like, and which she could convince herself might be even worse than it seemed: those occasional flashes of anger.

I wondered if he might be dangerous, she reminded herself. She pushed aside all benefit of the doubt and tried to feed her worst possible imaginings. *He's charismatic. He could secretly be a psychopath. That's definitely not incompatible with Gemini.*

She pictured Xander as the psychopathic villain of one of those suspense movies she had seen on one of her many dates. Scarily, it wasn't that hard. Xander's personality and the one the villain had shown in public weren't that dissimilar.

He has very little control over himself. He knows he's doomed. He has nothing to live for, and nothing to lose. Isn't that the sort of person who could easily become an ax murderer?

Lucy's heart raced. She was starting to believe that it might be true. Why hadn't she seen this before? She should never have started to trust him in the first place!

"Are you kidding me?!" a voice exploded from downstairs.

Lucy's eyes flew open.

"LUCY!" her father bellowed from below. "Get down here!"

She ran down the stairs, tripping twice in her haste. She barely saved herself from a twisted ankle by seizing the handrail.

Her father was standing in the living room with a purple face and a crumpled piece of paper in his hand.

"This!" he shouted, waving it at Xander, who was lounging against the wall and smirking. "THIS!"

"What is it, Dad?" Lucy asked, carefully avoiding looking at Xander. She didn't want to undo all her hard work.

"I asked a perfectly reasonable question about his intentions," Lucy's father bellowed, "and he said, 'I'll draw my feelings for Lucy!' and then he drew *THIS!*"

He thrust the crumpled ball of paper in Xander's direction.

The guy cackled.

"What is it?" Lucy asked curiously, reaching for it.

"You're not looking at it!" her dad screamed, wrenching the ball of paper away. "It's obscene! And *you!* Get out of my house! Never come back!"

"Sorry, sweet lips," Xander said with a mocking sneer so cold that it made chills run down Lucy's back. "Guess it won't work out between us. Oh, what a shame."

He made a rude gesture, barged past them, and headed out the front door. There was a sound of keys in the ignition of a motorcycle, then the roar of it leaving.

Lucy shuddered, feeling like she'd dodged a bullet. If that had been his first reaction to losing his feelings for her . . . well, that showed his true colors, all right.

Of course, he might have done something completely against his character in order to make it easier for her to stay disgusted with him because he was a nice guy . . . but no, she shouldn't give him the benefit of the doubt. That kind of thinking was dangerous.

Not Quite a Choice

"Well, there goes my ride home," Alex commented, coming out of the kitchen and glancing out the front window. "And Catherine and your wife are still too busy talking about what to name the columns to even start the meeting. I don't suppose you could drive me back after we've finished?"

Lucy's father breathed heavily, face still red with outrage. "Only if you promise to make sure that — that — *thing* stays away from my daughter forever!"

"Yes, that's easily promised," Alex said calmly. "I don't want them dating, either."

Lucy sniffed and gave Alex a chilly look as she walked past him. He seemed inordinately pleased about that. It was a good thing she disliked him so much, since her ever being attracted to Alex again would also affect Xander.

Soon after that, Steven arrived, apologizing for being half an hour late and blaming traffic. Then the meeting of all the cursed finally started.

It was every bit as interminable as Lucy had expected. They made her take eight billion personality quizzes, and Catherine had way too many ideas about how to compile them into a useful scoring rubric.

Lucy's eyes glazed over during a discussion about whether "impulsive" or "flighty" should be combined into one trait or kept separate. It was so boring that she was beginning to long for her math homework —

Wait! No! No, she wasn't!

There was only one thing for a self-respecting not-wanting-to-turn-into-Virgo to do.

"I'm leaving to go see my friend Carrie," Lucy announced, standing. "Have fun with your charts and things."

"*Lucy!*" her mother exclaimed, looking outraged.

"Wait, no!" Steven said, pointing to one of the columns on the spreadsheet. "That's exactly the sort of behavior she should be exhibiting if she's trying to resist being changed!"

Lucy's mother stared at the color-coded spreadsheet on her laptop, then at Lucy, clearly torn about what the right answer was.

"Okay, fine," she said reluctantly. "Go have fun with Carrie."

Trying not to grin too broadly, Lucy grabbed the car keys out of her mother's purse and headed out to the car, pulling her phone out of her pocket to call Carrie.

An ironclad excuse to get out of all responsible and dull things? she thought, unlocking the car. *Sure! Twist my arm!*

It was nice to have some advantages to being cursed.